THE GIANT AND THE MOUSE

by

Sandra Saer

illustrated by

Martin Hargreaves

UNIVERSITY C.

AUTHOR:

TITLE:

DATE: 2/04

ST/SAE

D0281947

SUBJECT: CR

British Library Cataloguing in Publication Data

**A catalogue record for this book is available
from the British Library**

ISBN 0 9534611 2 2

© Sandra Saer

All rights reserved. No part of this publication
may be reproduced, stored in a retrieval system,
or transmitted in any form or by any means, electronic,
mechanical, photocopying, recording, or otherwise,
without the prior permission of the publisher.

First published 2003, by
SMH BOOKS
Pear Tree Cottage, Watersfield, Pulborough,
West Sussex, RH20 1NG
Tel. 01798 831260

Typeset by Michael Walsh
MusicPrint, Warblington

Printed and bound in Great Britain by
RPM Reprographics, Chichester

For my Children,
Angus, Ben, Orlando and Bella
(especially for Ben, who provided the initial inspiration)
and
for my Grandchildren,
Amelia, Toby, Thomas, Isabel and Charis,
with much love to all nine.

CONTENTS

Chapter 1

GETTING TOGETHER

It is not easy to imagine a giant and a mouse living together. But I know a giant and a mouse who did. They had lived under the same roof for as long as their friends and neighbours could remember. So long, that even the giant and the mouse had forgotten when, and how, they had met. They only remembered that it was at a time when they were both thinking of moving. So they decided to move together.

They built a house which looked rather like a kneesock, standing up. But instead of being made of wool or cotton or nylon, it was made of yellow brick, with a roof of wavy red tiles and a stone chimney.

The house had to be very large, of course, to fit the giant. It wouldn't have been any good – would it? – building a house for a mouse and *hoping* the giant would be able to get in. He certainly would *not* have been able to. So, for the mouse, it was a very big house indeed.

The giant's bedroom was downstairs, at the front of the house. They shared a kitchen and sitting room at the back.

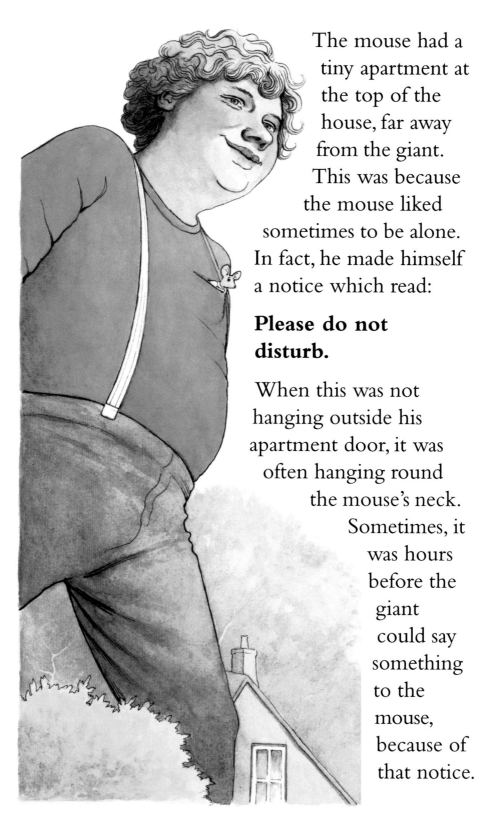

The mouse had a tiny apartment at the top of the house, far away from the giant. This was because the mouse liked sometimes to be alone. In fact, he made himself a notice which read:

Please do not disturb.

When this was not hanging outside his apartment door, it was often hanging round the mouse's neck. Sometimes, it was hours before the giant could say something to the mouse, because of that notice.

The other reason for the mouse's rooms being at the top was that, at night, the giant often snored. The noise was so loud that even right up there, with his windows tight shut, the walls lined with foam mattresses, and cotton wool plugs in his ears, the mouse could still hear the snoring.

Their house was on the edge of a green wood, on a little hill behind the village. The trees gave cool shade in the summer, and sheltered them against the wind and the rain in winter. Wood for their fires was scattered all around.

The house was in the middle of a garden, full of good things to eat, and bright, sweet-smelling flowers for the bees to get their honey from.

The village was just near enough for the giant to reach in one stride, to do any shopping the mouse might need.

It *was* strange that the giant and the mouse got on well, for they were as different from each other as chalk and cheese.

The giant was especially large. People and animals who didn't know him were frightened by his size, and ran away from him as fast as they possibly could. Folk hurried into their homes, squirrels jumped into their hollows. Birds flew up into the highest branches of trees, and rabbits hopped quickly back into their burrows.

But people and animals who <u>knew</u> the giant were not a bit afraid of him. They knew that he was the gentlest and kindest giant in the world. He didn't behave a bit like other giants we know about. He didn't eat people, or throw them into prison. He didn't fly into roaring rages and knock down houses that stood in his way.

In fact, as a giant, he was a bit of a joke. The mouse certainly thought so. He was always laughing at the giant…Well, not so much laughing as going "Huh!" at him, to show how silly he thought the giant was. But the giant didn't mind. He was happy-go-lucky. He loved to have fun, and enjoyed very simple games, like rolling down slopes, counting buttercups in the field, sitting and imagining things in the flames of the sitting-room fire, and pretending his bed was a boat and rowing it all round the world at night. He wasn't much good at housework, but the mouse was, so that didn't matter.

The mouse was extremely houseproud. He liked to have everywhere tidy and shining, clean and sweet-smelling. Even if he was tired out at the end of the day, he always finished washing up, plumped up the cushions, and brushed crumbs of bread off the carpet, before going to bed. He enjoyed doing these things, although you would not have thought so, to hear him grumbling about the place. But then, he enjoyed grumbling, too.

On a hot, sunny day, he grumbled that the lettuces would die because they needed rain. If it rained, he would grumble that the path to the lettuces was wet and slippery. Even when the house was in order, the lettuces watered, the path dry, the giant well-behaved (!), the mouse would pace up and down EXPECTING something bad to happen.

When the mouse was in a bad mood, he looked terrible. His frown made thick lines on his forehead, his eyes narrowed into ugly slits, and his mouth set in a thin, hard line. And his bow tie would droop miserably. Even if he was in a good mood, he rarely smiled. He found it difficult to smile.

But the mouse had his good points. Great in the house and in the garden. Very sensible. He never got in a panic.

The mouse was all things the giant was not. No doubt that is why they got along somehow, and lived together for such a long time.

Chapter 2

THE GIANT'S WASHING DAY

One day, the giant was in such a helpful mood that he said to the mouse:

"I'm going to do all our washing today. Every bit, mouse."

"Well," said the mouse, not showing he was pleased, "get on with it!"

So the giant collected his things, which made a very large pile, and the mouse's things, which made just a small pile, and he put them in the large dustbin they used for washing clothes. He filled the dustbin with water out of an enormous kettle left to him by his Grandmother Huge, threw in a boxful of washing powder, and swished it all round with a great wooden spoon he had carved out of a plank. He washed and rinsed, and squeezed out everything, singing as he did so.

He could see the sun shining outside, where he soon would be, and he felt good *inside* because he was being so helpful. The mouse would be pleased, although he wouldn't show it.

At last, he had hung out all the washing on the line in the yard. Then he went away and completely forgot about it. He went down to the field at the bottom of the garden to count buttercups. He often spent hours and hours there, just counting buttercups. It was a very peaceful thing to do.

As the day wore on, the sky grew greyer and greyer. The giant was having such a marvellous time, he didn't notice. But the mouse did. Looking cross, he marched across the field to giant, who was lying on back with his legs crossed, with counted buttercups thrown all round him.

"Look," said the mouse, "can't you see the sky is getting black?"

"Mmmmm?" replied the giant, absent-mindedly. "One, two, three, four, five – Oh! So it is! It's getting black all right. It's going to rain, don't you think?" "Yes, I *do* think," said the mouse. "What are you going to do with *your* washing?"

"Well, yes, I suppose I'd better get it in. But first of all, I think I'll come in and sit by the fire for a bit, and have a cup of tea. Will you make us one, or shall I?" This was quite clever of him, because the mouse

hated the mess the giant
always made in the kitchen,
and always said "Oh, I'll
make the tea. You go and
sit down."

The mouse went off to
make the tea, and the giant sat by the fire, and put
his slippers on. It was a lovely fire. The giant looked
and saw many different colours all at once in the
flames: orange and yellow and red and black and
grey and brown, mixed up together and changing
shape all the time. One minute the fire was yellow
and a little bit orange, then it was just black because
the flames had died down. Suddenly there was a
swoosh of grey smoke out of a gassy piece of coal,
and it was all witchy and funny. Then the flames
came back, and the fire was orange and yellow
again, then red, glowing and beautiful.

The giant sat in the warmth, thinking it was nice to
be in, and away from the buttercups for a while.

The mouse wheeled in his cup of tea, sighing.
"Here you are." He said. "One of these days, I
suppose *you'll* get the tea. Maybe tomorrow..." He
stood there for at least a minute, tutting and
muttering unpleasantly.

The giant didn't take a scrap of notice. "Mouse,
thank you *so* much. What a lovely cup of tea that looks!

Mmmmm!"
And into his cup, the
size of a bucket, he
emptied a packet of sugar and four
bottles of cold, white milk. Outside, the sky went
from black to purple. It looked bruised all over.

The mouse, looking out of the window, said "Now
look, if you don't get that washing in, it'll get all wet
again, and what a waste of time…"

"Yes, yes," agreed the giant, gently, "I know. I
promise…in a minute."

But then, something terrible happened. The giant,
warmed and full of sleep by the fire, forgot he had
promised to do something. He forgot about the
washing. He simply went to bed.

The night sky grew blacker and blacker, and the
rain witches, screeching merrily, whizzed around,

piercing all the clouds with their closed umbrellas, and then opening the umbrellas very quickly indeed, to save themselves from getting wet. It was a game they played. Afterwards, they counted up to see who had pierced the most clouds, and the winner was given a special golden umbrella for being so clever.

Down came the rain, and everything got soaked – including the washing.

Next morning, the mouse was bustling about early, as usual. He had forgotten about the washing, too. But it was the first thing the giant thought about when he woke up.

"Oh, Golly Moses!" he moaned, "it must be dripping wet. What am I going to do? What is the mouse going to say? How will I get the things dry again?" He tried to put on a big smile when he went down for breakfast, so that the mouse wouldn't see how worried he was.

"Good morning, mouse," he said, not *too* cheerily.

The mouse, who had cleaned the most of the house while the giant was still asleep, sighed and tutted hard. "Good *morning*! More like afternoon. Sit down. Here's your breakfast. Hurry up, so that I can clear away before lunchtime!"

After breakfast, the giant went to the kitchen window and looked carefully out. You know how you look out of a window when you want it to be fine, after it has been raining. You look with one eye slightly open, because you're frightened at first to open both eyes to the weather.

Anyway, it seemed brighter, so the giant bravely opened one eye a little wider. Then he opened both eyes and looked out…He smiled a very wide smile indeed at what he saw. For it was most beautiful day. The blue sky had not a cloud in it, and the sun shone everywhere.

He thought: Now, if the day stays like that – shiny, sunny and warm, in a few hours' time, the washing is going to be dry again. If I can just keep the mouse busy for the morning, keep him from thinking about the washing, it'll be all right. The wash will be dry, and he'll think I remembered it last night, and pegged it all out again this morning. Then he won't be cross. I so *hate* him being cross.

He managed to keep the mouse busy all morning, doing things. The mouse went round grumbling, saying "Why don't *you* do that?" and the giant said "But you do it so much *better* than I do,"…"Won't *you* do the dishes? They look so much more sparkly when you do them,"…"Why don't *you* scrub the table?"…"You iron our shirts, then?"…"Won't you at least make your bed?" asked the mouse. "But *you*," said the giant, "make it so much more *comfortable* than I could ever do."

Meanwhile, a brown stew was bubbling in its black pot on the fire. The giant thought it smelled delicious and knew it must be nearly lunchtime.

The time had come to go out and feel the washing on the line.

He was rather worried, in case it was still wet, so he went backwards out into the courtyard. He put a big hand out behind him and touched the end of the first thing on the line, which happened to be a towel. It was as dry as a bone, and warm, too. Well, the giant knew that since the towel was dry, then everything else must be dry, too, because towels — being thick — usually take the longest time to dry.

The giant was so pleased that he yelled "YIPPEE!" loudly, and the chimney jumped off the roof, in astonishment. The giant put it carefully back again. He then took all the washing off the line, clipping the pegs along the bottom of his sweater. He took the dry things into the kitchen, whistling softly between his teeth."

All he said to the mouse was "Well, here we are," and all the mouse said to the giant was "Good.

About time you came in. Wash your hands, and dry them properly. Lunch is ready."

Whew! thought the giant. Thank goodness for that!

Chapter 3

THE MIDNIGHT FEAST

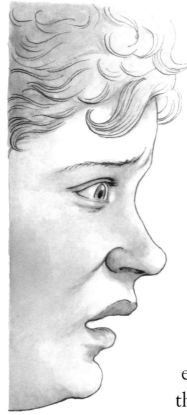

"Giant," said the mouse sternly, one evening, "we are getting fat." "Oh, I don't think so. I don't think *I'm* fat," said the giant, "and I'm sure *you're* not," he added politely.

"Perhaps not – yet," said the mouse. "But I'm going to be! I shall soon be so fat, I won't be able to walk. It's these GIGANTIC meals you have every day. It makes *me* eat more than I should."

"Well, I <u>am</u> a giant, you know," he said. "I need lots of food to fill up all the corners."

"I'm sure you eat *too much,* giant or no," said the mouse. "I've been reading all about it in *Mousey Mousey Magazine*. It says once you start getting fat, it's hard to stop."

"Fiddlesticks!" said the giant. "I could stop any time."

"Well, I'm glad to hear that," said the mouse. "Because we're stopping TODAY." The mouse spread out their red and white checked tablecloth, and laid it. No cups, no sugar bowl, no milk…

"What about a nice cup of tea?" suggested the giant, pulling a face. "Oh go on, mousey-mouse. Just one last cup."

"DON'T CALL ME MOUSEY-MOUSE! You can have lemon juice with no sugar in your tea. That seems to be all right."

"Oooof, how horrid!" said the giant, pulling a face. "I think I'd rather have water."

"Fine." The mouse nodded. "Have water instead."

The mouse wheeled a jug of water over to the giant. He put on the table some cream crackers, unbuttered, a bowl of lettuce, two tomatoes – one large, one small – two pieces of cheese – both large (being a mouse, he *loved* cheese), and a plateful of sliced oranges.

Unhappily, the giant sat down and looked at the meal spread before him.

"But that's just a snack," he protested. "That will only fill *one tiny* corner."

"You must be brave," said the mouse, tucking his napkin into his shirt. "Tell yourself you're not at all hungry, and that you only need a little something to keep you going until tomorrow."

"Until tomorrow!" The giant stared in horror at the mouse, but the mouse went on calmly nibbling his cracker and cheese, as if nothing at all was the matter.

After tea, the giant, who was really hungry, said to the mouse: "I'll do the washing up, if you like. It won't take me a minute."

The mouse, however, knew that all the giant wanted to do was to creep into the larder when his back was turned. In there, was a delicious leg of smoked ham he had bought that day in the village. He had also bought two loaves of crumbly brown bread, a packet of butter, a large jar of heather honey – and a few tasty bits and pieces he knew they both enjoyed. It was to have been a special treat, for later.

But the mouse would allow no tricks.

"It's all right," he said to the giant, "it won't take *me* a minute, either! I'm used to it. You go and sit down by the fire."

Very sad, very fed up – and very hungry, the giant did as he was told. Soon after, the mouse joined him. They sat for a while by the fire, not talking much, just reading. The giant had real hunger pains in his tummy. Even the mouse, small though he was, felt the need for something else to eat. He went to the kitchen, and came back with a plate. On it, were two cream crackers – unbuttered.

The giant looked at the crackers, miserably. "Thank you, mouse," he groaned, taking one. "You're VERY kind."

"Well, since we're not having hot chocolate tonight. I thought we'd better having something else now."

The giant got to his feet, very suddenly.

"I do wish you wouldn't do that," said the mouse, tut-tutting and looking up, up, up at him. "You make me jump."

"NO HOT CHOCOLATE! Well, that's it. I might as well go to bed. At least I can *dream* about food. I suppose *that* is allowed?" he asked the mouse, glowering at him as he did so.

"Oh perfectly," said the mouse calmly. "Sweet dreams!"

The giant lumbered off. "Sweet dreams, indeed!" he said to himself as he got into his red-and-blue-striped pyjamas. Usually, the pyjamas cheered him up when he went to bed feeling sad or ill. They were so bright and jolly. Sometimes he felt he should wear them all day, not just in bed.

(One morning, he had gone down to breakfast in his pyjamas. "Nobody eats at this table unless he is dressed," the mouse had said, angrily. "Off you go! Get dressed, and hurry up about it. The eggs are getting cold."

Now the giant sat on his bed. Not even his pyjamas could comfort him. "Oh, pyji-pyji-jamas," he whispered sadly to them, as he buttoned the jacket, "what am I going do?"

When he had finished his usual prayers, the giant added a special one. "Please let the mouse forget all about our being fat, tomorrow. Amen."

He climbed into bed, but he couldn't sleep. He turned the light back on and read a comic. Then he read one of his favourite adventure stories. "That's bound to take my mind off food," he told himself. But it didn't.

He put out the light again, and lay down. He did doze off, and he had a lovely dream about the big round orange blossom bush in the garden. The food witch had waved the black stick in her fat brown hand, and covered the bush with oranges, as well as apples, cream cakes, roast beef, pickled onions, honey sandwiches, and 'squashed-fly' biscuits, until the branches were so heavy with good things to eat, they almost touched the ground.

The giant woke up just as he was about to reach for a specially creamy cream cake.

"Oh," he cried, unhappily, flopping back on his pillows, "I was only dreaming."

For a long time, he lay there, looking out of the window. He watched the silver stars playing 'Now I twinkle, now I don't', in the black sky, and tried to tell himself that he could wait until breakfast. But it was no good.

He got up, and crept towards the kitchen. He made no noise at all, and was just about to turn the handle of the kitchen door, slowly and quietly, when a tiny screech made him start in terror.

"Ouch! Why don't you look where you're going!" It was the mouse. Although the giant didn't ask, and the mouse

didn't explain, they both knew that he, like the giant, was just too hungry to wait until morning.

Without a word, the mouse set the table. The giant went to the larder, and brought out most of what was in it – roast ham, bread, butter, honey, pickled onions, 'squashed-fly' biscuits, potato crisps, oranges and apples, a large bag of cream cakes, and a bottle of apple juice.

They sat down and ate and ate, until almost EVERYTHING on that table had disappeared. Then they drank down the cold, pale golden apple juice. Finally, full to bursting, each put his head down on the table, and slept.

Morning came, but all was quiet in the house of the giant and the mouse. Birds whistled as they got on with their chores. Squirrels stored their nuts. Flowers opened in the sunshine. A mouse newsboy dropped a copy of the *Mouse Times* through the letterbox. The farmer left a churn of fresh, creamy milk at the gate. Still no sound.

The clock cuckoo came out and cuckoo'd crazily for as long as he wanted: on the hour, at a quarter-past. At half-past and at a quarter-to. It was he who finally woke up the giant and the mouse. He got bored at being able to cuckoo as much as he liked *all* the time, with no one popping him back into his little hut, and slamming the door. So, at eleven o'clock, he cuckoo'd very loudly and long, and ended up going 'Yoohoo!' in such an extraordinary way that both mouse and giant heard him.

"Where are we? What on earth?…In the kitchen? At the table? IN OUR PYJAMAS!" The mouse couldn't believe his eyes.

"We were hungry, that's what," said the giant. He went to the larder. "We must have been *very* hungry," he said. "There's scarcely anything left in there."

The mouse giggled, which was not something he did often.

"I remember now," he said. "*Mousey Mousey Magazine*, and the cream crackers."

The giant laughed. "Wasn't it a wonderful midnight feast, though, Mousey? It was almost worth having such an *awful* tea."

But what shall we have for breakfast?" asked the mouse, trying to stop giggling and be sensible.

"Breakfast!" exclaimed the giant. "After that, I shan't want to eat a thing for two days."

And he didn't.

Chapter 4

THE GIANT: PAINTER AND DECORATOR

"Mouse," said the giant one morning, as they were having breakfast, "I have a simply marvellous idea. Shall I tell you about it?"

"I suppose you'd better," said the mouse, without interest. "But finish your breakfast first, before it gets cold."

But the giant couldn't wait to finish breakfast. He was much too excited.

"I must tell you NOW, mouse. It's such a good idea. I've had it several times this week, but never so GOOD as this morning."

"Well," said the mouse, sighing, "get on with it, then. What is this 'good idea'?"

"I'm going to paint the house."

"Oh *no!*" groaned the mouse. "But you only painted it two years ago, and I still haven't got used to all those terrible bright colours."

"Now that summer's come, the sun shines into every corner of the house. And some of the corners are dirty and dusty. And the colours have faded a lot, you know."

"Thank goodness they *have* faded, although not half as much as I would have liked," said the mouse, shortly. "I have never got used to having a red room with an orange ceiling!"

"I know," said the giant, nodding and smiling kindly. "That's why I want to paint it again."

The mouse just said "Mmmmm", and finished his milk.

There was silence for a minute. The mouse was wondering what horrible colours the giant would paint his bedroom next, and the giant was thinking of all the lovely cheery colours he could use ALL OVER THE HOUSE.

"We'll start with the kitchen," said the giant, so suddenly that the mouse nearly fell off his stool.

"Oh yes?" said the mouse, coldly, sitting straight again.

"Yes. The kitchen will have red and yellow stripes with a green ceiling. And nice white paint on the door and window. You do like white paint, don't you?"

"Yes, at least I like white paint," agreed the mouse. He had closed his eyes in horror at the thought of working in a kitchen full of red and yellow stripes.

"Then," said the giant, "after the kitchen, I'll do the sitting room."

"And what will you do to the sitting room?" asked the mouse, re-opening his eyes.

"Black!" said the giant, looking terribly excited. "Wouldn't that be gorgeous?"

"Gorgeous! I think it would be quite <u>awful</u>! What's the matter with the way it is? Pale grey with that nice red rug on the floor?"

"Oh, but you've got to *change* things, mouse," cried the giant. "You don't always want to have your sitting room the same colour. Just think. When you come in and sit down in the evening, it'll be like being in a new room."

"But – black!" said the mouse, with a gulp.

"Yes. Black walls and ceiling. Black carpet, black chairs, black everything. Won't that be fun?"

"Fun!" snorted the mouse. "It sounds *very* funny to me! I've never heard anything like it. A black room? It'll be like sitting outside in the night, only we'll be inside. It will give me a very *funny* feeling..."

"When that's done, there's your bedroom."

"And what," said the mouse, covering his face, "are you going to paint that?"

"Ah well," said the giant, "I know exactly what. I'm going to get some of that yellow paper with red Mr Happy faces all over it. All those round faces with big smiles. It'll make you get up in the morning in a much better temper. You won't come down groaning 'I've got to get the breakfast — again!' No, instead you'll say 'Ooooh, what a lovely day! What can I make for breakfast? Something really special to please old Gianty-giant. Lovely crisp, brown toast. Lovely crackly pink bacon. And some of that yummy green-orange marmalade he likes so much."

"Shut up!" snapped the mouse.

"Now, now," scolded the giant, "…and when I've done your room, I'll do mine."

"And what, dare I ask, will you do with your room?"

A really bright gleam came into the giant's eye. "I'm going to paint it white—" The mouse breathed a sigh of relief.

"— and then," the giant went on (and the mouse sat up straight once more, startled, "I'll…I'll get out my paint box with all the different colours in it —

green and black, purple and yellow, blue and red, and everything, and I'll just throw bits of paint all over the walls. I'll put my hand in the purple paint and go 'Peeeeew!' and I'll have lots of lovely purple spots. Then I'll put my hand in the yellow paint and go 'Peeeeew!' and I'll have lots of yellow splodges. Then I'll put—"

"Please, *please*," squeaked the mouse, "don't go on. I can't stand it."

"After that, I'm going to spot paint all over the walls of our bathrooms."

But the mouse didn't wait to hear about the bathrooms. Hands to his ears, he rushed up to his sitting room. There, he sat down to have a hard think. What could he do to stop the giant? There must be something. There was! He went back to the kitchen.

"I've got a good idea, too, giant. I suggest – that we leave the whole house the way it is."

"O-o-o-oh! Don't be so stick-in-the-mud."

"Now,"
said the
mouse
firmly. "you're
going to promise me that you
won't do any of the terrible things
to the house that you've been telling me about. If
you don't promise, I'll—"

"You'll what?" asked the giant, in a sulk.

"I won't make you any more breakfast, or lunch, or
tea. I won't make your bed, darn your socks, or
mend the fire. I won't do another thing for you. I
warn you."

So the giant had to promise. And the mouse went
off to make the beds, thanking his lucky stars that
he had been able to make the giant see sense.

The giant was really miserable. He'd had all these
marvellous dreams, and all the mouse could do was
make him promise not to do anything about them.
It just wasn't fair. He wouldn't break his promise,
because he knew that would be wrong. But he was
very upset, and for a long time he sat sipping his tea
(which by now was cold and horrid), and feeling
sorry for himself But *suddenly*, a big grin lit up his
face.

"Ahaaaaaaah!" he cried out, merrily. "But I didn't
tell mouse what I was going to do with the front

hall. So I didn't promise *not* to do anything with *that*!"

He painted the hall bright red. Then he got a pot of black paint, dipped his great giant's hand in it and put giant handmarks all over the red walls and ceiling. When he had finished, he went out into the field to count buttercups, whistling a happy tune.

"Hee, hee, hee!" he laughed, making the bees rush off in all directions at the noise. "That'll fix old mouse. What *will* he say?"

Suddenly, he heard a terrible 'Aaaaaaaaah!' in the house and, he thought "That's it. Mousey has seen my black handmarks in the hall. Now for the fun!"

The mouse came scurrying out of the house, through the garden, across the field to the giant. One of his ears was pressed close to his head — a sure sign that he was furiously angry. Snorting with rage, he ripped a buttercup, root and all, from the ground. He waved it menacingly in front of the giant's face, and screamed:

"Oooooooooooh!"

Chapter 5

THE GIANT'S MAY BIRTHDAY

It was a fine warm evening in May. The giant and the mouse were in their sitting room, drinking tea. They were not quarrelling. They were not even talking. Just resting peacefully for a little, before going to bed. A sweet-smelling little pinewood fire burned orange and gold in the grate. A pile of newly-made buttered toast was propped up in the hearth.

Suddenly, the giant jumped up from his chair and cried: "I've just remembered, mouse. It's my *birthday* tomorrow."

"I do wish you wouldn't do that," grumbled the mouse.

"Do what?"

"Suddenly jump up and shout like that. You know what a terrible noise you make when you're only *whispering*. When you shout – it's FRIGHTENING."

The mouse wasn't really frightened at all, even though the giant was so large and he was so small. He knew the giant was gentle and kind at heart, and wouldn't hurt a flea, let alone a mouse.

But the giant looked worried for a moment. "Mouse, I'm so sorry. How stupid of me!"

"Yes, it was," said the mouse, feeling better.

"Here, have another piece of toast," said the giant, and he handed a piece to the mouse, who took it and said "thank you".

"My birthday! Yippeeeee!" But the giant said "Yippeeeee!" very softly. The last time he had shouted it, not only the chimney but the roof had jumped off the house in surprise, with two terrible bumps. It was difficult having to whisper when you felt so full of joy because it would soon be your birthday, but that's what the giant had to do.

"I wonder what I'm going to have for my birthday," said the giant.

"Well, one thing you *need* is a pair of socks," said the mouse. "Just look at this one."

And he held up the end of one of the giant's bright pink socks, which he was trying to mend. It was full of holes.

"Three days it'll take me to mend this sock," he muttered. "Yes, you certainly should have socks for your birthday.

34

What colour would you like?"

"Oh, I don't want *socks* for my birthday! I want something much more interesting."

"Well," thought the mouse out loud, "let me see… Would you like some new sandals?"

The giant pulled a face. Socks? Sandals? That was not what he wanted at all. But he just said "I don't think there's enough money in the money box for sandals."

"Mmmm," said the mouse, looking at the giant over his steel-rimmed spectacles.

"Well, how about…? I know! I'll make you a nice picture tonight when you're in bed. Would you like that?"

The giant brightened up. "Yes, that would be very nice," he said, "because we could hang it on the wall in my bathroom, where there aren't any pictures. The walls look lonely without pictures."

The mouse and the giant finished up their buttered toast and had another cup of tea each. They talked for a long time about presents the giant might like, and presents he didn't really want. Then the giant went up to bed, leaving the mouse to darn another two feet of sock.

The giant wanted to get to bed early. He knew that the sooner he was asleep, the quicker his birthday would come.

Before he got into bed, he knelt down to say his prayers. They *were* prayers, but anyone listening might not have thought so. They would have thought he was just chatting to Someone, which he was.

"Hello, God," he said, "how are you this evening? Did you know it's my birthday tomorrow? Oh, before we talk about that, I must say thank you. I've had a really good day. Counting buttercups in the field, walking in the woods… And the mouse made a sugary apple pie for tea, which was delicious. Now, about tomorrow. As I said, it's my birthday. But of course, you know that already. I want to ask you something special. Are you listening, God?"

No sound, but the giant knew that God was listening, even though He said nothing.

"Well, God, this is what I want. I mean, what I would like. I would like the most beautiful May day You have ever made for anybody."

At that moment, the mouse was just passing the giant's door, and overheard him.

Well, he thought, that's a funny thing to ask for. Maybe it's rather a good idea. But it's going to be a fine day, any way. There's a red sunset. Silly fellow, that giant! (But he didn't say "silly fellow" at all crossly.)

The giant and the mouse slept.

Next morning, when he woke up, the giant jumped out of bed and went to the window. He opened the curtains wide and looked out.

And there it was. The most brilliant May day he had ever seen. Blue skies, a bright sun shining, green trees, the field yellow and glistening with uncounted buttercups, the garden bright with flowers. Beautiful!

The giant was so pleased, he almost cried. Instead, he ran back to his bed and, still in his red-and-blue-striped pyjamas, he knelt and said "Oh, *thank you*, God. That really is the most perfect present. You *are* good to me!" Then he went down to breakfast.

On the table, in his place, he found not only cards from his family and friends, but so many presents, he couldn't believe his eyes.

"Mouse! All I asked for was a May day, a lovely one, and I have not only that but all these marvellous presents, too." There were parcels of all shapes and sizes, wrapped up in red paper, yellow paper, mauve paper and stripey paper.

"Don't make me eat my breakfast," he begged the mouse. "I have to open all these things IMMEDIATELY."
And he did.

There was a pair of velvet-soft knitted socks from 'the Woolliest Sheep on the Hill'.

An alarm clock from sleepy old Mrs Dormouse.

(Someone had given her another one, with a much louder bell.) The White family of rabbits had sent him a fluffy talcum-powder puff (an extra tail they didn't need). And many more things. And – from the mouse, there was a rather dark picture, covered in dots.

"What a lovely – er – dotty picture," said the giant, with a grateful smile. "But why is it covered in dots, Mousey-mouse?"

"Well, you see, it's a rainy picture," explained the mouse. "I thought if I drew you a rainy picture, it would certainly be a sunny day today."

"I see," said the giant, "who didn't really see at all. He didn't understand quite what the mouse meant. Still, it was the thought that counted. And to please the mouse, he picked up the dotty picture as soon as he left the table, took it to his bedroom, and pinned it up on the wall.

After lunch, some of the giant's family

arrived to wish him "all the best". There was merry
Uncle Toby and quiet Aunt Maud, and their three
children, and Great Aunt Grace, who never smiled
but was a good old stick.

And there was mad Uncle Seamus. In spite of Aunt
Felicity being there, he kept turning everyone's hair
different colours, and disappearing, only to turn up
in a different place. But then, he *was* a wizard.

The giant made his family stay on the other side of
the wood from the house, in case they forgot to be
quiet and frightened the mice, rabbits and people,
whom he also loved. Even Uncle Seamus promised
to be as good as he could.

When it was time for the birthday party tea, after
playing musical bumps and hide–and–seek, the
giants – as quietly as possible – tiptoed over the
wood to the garden, and joined the people, mice,
rabbits and other smaller creatures for tea. Just
before the end, the mouse, helped by several of his
friends, wheeled out the birthday cake. It had
cherries and sultanas and all the giant's favourite
things inside. And it was covered with white icing
and had several candles on top. The mouse had
written in blue icing round the cake :
HAPPY BIRTHDAY GIANT.

And in fact, as the giant told God later, he did have
a very happy May birthday indeed.

Chapter 6

HOW THE LETTUCES GOT WEEDED

"Tell me, what would you do," the giant asked the mouse, "if you had a bad foot and you had to do some gardening?"

The mouse didn't reply. He was polishing their silver on the kitchen table – one enormous spoon, and one small one: the size of half a mustard spoon. And he was just at the best part – getting the silver polish off and putting a lovely shine on.

"Hey," said the giant, "did you hear what I said, Mousey?"

"Don't call me Mousey!" snapped the mouse. "I'm not a baby any more. Yes, I heard what you said."

"Well, then," the giant said again, "WHAT WOULD YOU DO?"

The mouse looked up, and saw that there was a speck of silver polish on one of his whiskers. He removed it carefully with one paw. Then he answered the giant's question.

"If I had a bad foot, I wouldn't do any gardening." The mouse had spoken!

"Oh that's a great help, that is," said the giant. "But I *have* to do some gardening. *Today!* If I don't get that lettuce patch weeded before the rain comes, the weeds will choke them."

"I'm not at all sure that it's going to rain today," said the mouse, looking out of the window. The sky was a clear, deep blue – the colour you always hope it will be when you go on holiday.

"It's going to rain. I know it," said the giant. "It may not look rainy, but I can smell the rain in the wind."

"But there isn't any wind today!" said the mouse, staring hard at the giant. "Really! Bright blue sky, and not even a breeze stirring the trees. And you say you must weed the lettuces, in spite of your bad foot, because there's rain in the wind? Mmmmm … I think you'd better go to bed and have a rest."

"I DON'T NEED –"

"A–a–a–a–a–," warned the mouse, "don't shout. *Please* don't shout."

So the giant whispered: "I don't need a rest."

"No, on second thoughts, you don't. You need your head examining." Which was rather a rude thing to say.

The giant looked at the mouse and the mouse, quite unafraid, looked at the giant. Neither of them said a word for quite a time. The cuckoo came out of the cuckoo clock and cuckoo'd gaily ten times before they noticed and shut him up again in his little house. (It was only two in the afternoon, after all.)

"It's not my head that needs looking at," said the giant, "it's my foot."

"Well, why on earth didn't you say so in the first place?" growled the mouse. "Come on outside, and I'll have a look."

The giant hobbled out into the garden, and lay down across the lawn. Shortly afterwards, the mouse came out. A large piece of cotton wool was sticking out of his apron pocket. In one paw, he carried a bowl of hot water. In the other paw, he had a magnifying glass, so that when he looked at the giant's foot, he could see more clearly.

The mouse then brought along his step ladder. "Which foot is it?" he asked.

The giant wiggled his right foot. "That one," he said.

"Aha," said the mouse. "Let's see."

He put the step ladder against the giant's right foot, and climbed up, looking through his magnifying glass as he went.

"Ah yes," he said at last. "I've got it."

Now the mouse knew that if he told the giant that he had quite a nasty deep cut on the sole of his foot

– and he had, the giant would be horrified. The giant was a real coward when it came to cuts, aching teeth, splinters of wood, and things like that. So the mouse simply said, untruthfully: "Oh, it's nothing much."

"Thank goodness for that." The giant sighed with relief. "It does hurt, though, mouse."

"All it needs is cleaning, a dab of ointment, and a nice big plaster on," soothed the mouse, quite pleasantly for him.

"A plaster!" said the giant, quite excited. He loved having plasters on, because everyone came up and said "What *have* you done? Is it bad?" And he could say "Oh, it's nothing really. Just a slight cut." And people would look at him in admiration, and go off murmuring

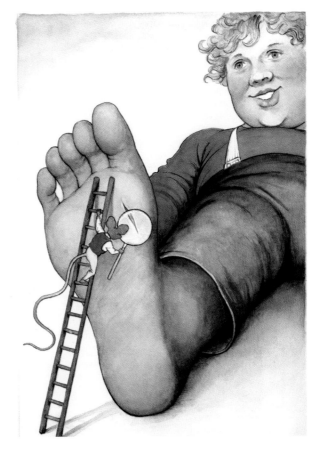

"Well – isn't he brave?"

"Yes, a plaster!" repeated the mouse, bringing him back to earth. "What a pity it won't show!"

"What? Oh, of course. It won't, will it?" The giant looked sadly disappointed.

"Never mind. The main thing is to cover the cut up, to keep the dirt out," said the mouse, sounding like a nurse. "There we are. All done." And he climbed down his ladder.

"Well, that feels much better," said the giant. "Thank you very much, Mousey – I mean, mouse. I suppose now there's nothing to stop me weeding the lettuces?"

"Nothing at all," said the mouse, with what the giant thought was a rather odd smile. The mouse know that, whether it rained or not, the lettuces *had* to be weeded. And since the giant wanted to do it, and didn't know how bad his cut was, well, why not let him get on with it?

And the giant did. He worked very hard for the rest of the afternoon, weeding, weeding, weeding. By teatime, it was all done. There were rows and rows of shining, pale green lettuces looking extremely comfortable in their clean bed of brown earth.

The giant stood up, and stretched. "Ooooh, my back!" he sighed, forgetting for a moment about his foot. He went inside, washed his hands and then sat down in front of a lovely fire. (The mouse lit a fire for the giant, every day of the year. In summer, and this was summer, they were cosy little fires – just a cheery glow to warm one's toes by.)

The mouse brought in some tea. "All finished?" he asked.

"Yes, all finished," said the giant.

"Well done!" praised the mouse.

"Well done?" The giant looked at the mouse quickly. "You've never said that to me before."

"I think," said the mouse slowly, "that considering you have a VERY NASTY cut on your foot, you've done very well indeed."

"But you said it was nothing at all," said the giant, now feeling his foot carefully.

"Of course I did! You've put off weeding those lettuces for far too long."

But the giant didn't hear that.

Knowing that he had a *bad* cut on his foot, he suddenly felt very ill indeed, and groaning "I must go to bed", to bed he went. That night, it rained hard. Everything in the garden, including the lettuces, drank up the rain, feeling much better, bigger and stronger for it.

The mouse was most surprised at the rain. The giant, huddled up under the bedclothes with his bad foot, didn't even notice it.

For three days, the mouse took the giant his meals in bed. Then one morning, he came in, ripped off the giant's plaster and said: "It's all healed. You can get up now."

"Oh I don't know," said the giant, doubtfully, "I still don't feel too good." In fact, he had had a fabulous time, lying in his comfortable bed, being looked-after by the mouse, and not having to do a thing.

But the mouse had had enough. "Nonsense!" he said firmly to the giant. "You're fine. Get up. Lunch in the kitchen in one hour."

"Oh, all right," said the giant. "What *is* for lunch?"

To the giant's astonishment, the mouse winked at him, broadly. "Among other things," he said, "lettuce!"

Chapter 7

TO THE SEA, BY CARPET

"Oh dear!" said the mouse, "what am I to do? It would be so nice, but I just can't. Oh dear, what a pity!"

The mouse was very upset. All morning, as he washed the dishes, made the beds, dusted the sitting room and peeled the potatoes for lunch, he kept saying "Oh dear, what a pity!" and things like that.

The giant spent most of that morning indoors. It was raining. He read some of his favourite books, played snap with himself, and blew bubbles. And all the time, he kept hearing the mouse mutter "Oh dear, oh dear, what a pity!"

At last, the giant just had to ask: "What is it, mouse? Is there anything I can do?"

"No, no. It's just that – dear, oh dear!" The mouse sniffed. "And I was so looking forward to it!"

"Looking forward to what?" the giant asked.

"Well, it's the church mouse outing to Goldensands on Saturday. And I did so want to go."

"Well, what's to stop you going?" demanded the giant, beating himself at noughts and crosses.

"Couldn't you come, too?" asked the mouse, sighing.

"You know very well I wouldn't fit into the coach with all you mice," said the giant. "But there's nothing to stop you going without me, Mouseymouse. Nothing at all."

"I suppose not," agreed the mouse. But to be quite truthful, the mouse, even though he spent a lot of time shouting at the giant, was fond of him. And he hated going anywhere without him.

That night, as they sipped hot chocolate by the fire, the mouse said: "Of course, I *could* go on the church mouse outing by myself. And it'd be nice to get away from *you* for a day, it certainly would! But *you* need a day at the seaside, too."

"Do I?" said the giant, getting up and looking at himself in the mirror.

"Yes, you do," said the mouse. "So I know what we'll do. We'll take the magic carpet.

The giant choked over his chocolate. "Oh no!" he shouted, just loud enough to make the clock jump up and down again on the mantelpiece. "That dreadful carpet! NO!"

"Why ever not?"

"You know very well, mouse, that wherever you say you want to go, the magic carpet will always take you somewhere else. He hates to do what anybody wants."

"But we can both *fit* on the carpet," argued the mouse.

The giant shook his head. The carpet had been a present from his Uncle Seamus, the wild one in the giant's family. The giant loved Uncle Seamus, who told wonderful stories, and could close his eyes and fly up in the air whenever he wanted to, because he was a wizard.

But the giant did not like the magic carpet. Even rolled up in the carpet house they had built specially for it, the carpet was

not to be trusted. Suddenly, as you walked in, it would unroll itself very quickly, and knock you – boom!

– against the wall. If you sat down on it, rolled up, it would wriggle, and make you fall off. And if you ever asked it to take you for a ride, well, anything could happen.

Next morning, the giant, who didn't want to disappoint the mouse, went along to have a little chat with the carpet. He told it that they wanted to go to the mountains, probably NOT on Saturday. They wished to be taken VERY SLOWLY, because they didn't want to spend long in the mountains enjoying themselves…

What he really meant was that they wanted to go to the seaside, yes, on Saturday, as quickly as possible, so that they could spend a lovely, long day there, lazing about.

"All right, mouse," said the giant at lunch, telling the mouse about his chat with the carpet, "we'll risk it. But don't blame me if things go wrong."

Saturday dawned bright and sunny. After breakfast, the mouse made cheese sandwiches and put them in a picnic hamper with honey cakes, salted peanuts, rosy red apples, and a bottle of lemonade to share. He also packed a white tablecloth and two red-and-white-checked napkins, fruit knives, a very large cup and a very small beaker, and a bag full of stale bread for the seabirds. The mouse liked to do things properly.

The giant dragged the magic carpet out of its house, and unrolled it. Then he and the mouse sat on the carpet, holding on to the hamper between them.

"Now!" commanded the giant, "take us to the mountains, VERY SLOWLY."

Quick as a flash, the carpet was up in the air, heading for the sea, and they arrived at Goldensands long before the church mouse outing's coach. The carpet came down behind a sandhill. When the giant and the mouse climbed off and rolled the carpet up again, they forgot all about it.

But the carpet heard the giant laugh gleefully, and say "Hee, hee, hee! That fooled the silly old carpet-carpet. And it thought it was being so clever. So here we are, mouse, all set to have a lovely day, *just* where we wanted to be!"

The carpet was furious. It would show them…

Before lunch, the giant and the mouse each made a sandcastle on the beach. The giant made an enormous one, like a house, and the mouse made a small one, the size of a matchbox. They were both very fine castles indeed.

Then they ran into the water, which was blue and warm and frothy with white waves breaking on it. They splashed and shouted, and had a wonderful time.

While the giant lay in the sun, getting dry, the mouse got their lunch out of the hamper, and laid it carefully on the white cloth on the sand. They ate up all the food, every scrap. And they finished with the fizzy lemonade, licking their lips with pleasure.

They were sitting a little way from the church-outing mice, because the giant didn't want to disturb them. After lunch, the mouse hurried off to say 'hello' to his friends and family. He made another small sandcastle with them, before going back to the giant.

All too soon, it was time to pack and go home. The giant and the mouse rolled out the magic carpet together, and sat down on it again, with the hamper between them.

Then they made a terrible mistake. They were so warm and sleepy, so full of sunshine, so happy and dreamy after all the fun they'd had at Goldensands, they just did not think.

"Now," ordered the giant, "take us home!"

But that was the last thing the magic carpet felt like doing. Having learnt that morning that the giant had tricked him into coming to the seaside, he was determined to teach the naughty fellow a lesson.

With a sudden 'whooooooosh!' he was away, up into the sky. The giant and the mouse had to grab each other, so as not to fall off.

And the carpet did NOT take them home! It took them high, high, up into the clouds. It took them through a storm, in which thunder roared like a house falling down, and lightning flashed so that they could hardly see, and the sky turned purple and black, as the rain poured down. They were soaked to the skin.

Then the carpet took them to the mountains, right up to the very peaks. They got covered in ice and snow, and the giant and mouse grew very cold indeed. So much so, that the giant put the mouse in his shirt pocket. He was much safer there, too.

The carpet was still angry. So next, it whizzed them off to Africa, where it was so hot that the mouse had to get out of the giant's pocket to try to cool off again.

The giant and the mouse were getting tired. They longed to be at home, tucked up in their warm beds. But they didn't dare to say to the carpet again "Take us home!" They knew that if they did, it wouldn't.

It was four in the morning when the carpet decided IT wanted to go home, and brought them down bang, smack, in the middle of their lawn. The mouse was so pleased to be back, he did a little jumpy, round-and-round dance all the way to the house. Then he went in, to make two cups of creamy hot chocolate. The giant rolled up the carpet and THREW him back into the carpet house. He was so cross, he didn't say "Thank you, carpet, for taking us to the seaside". He certainly didn't feel like saying "Thank you, carpet, for bringing us home through the mountains…and Africa!"

And I don't think anyone could blame him, do you?

Chapter 8

GETTING THE MOUSE AWAY

'What a silly thing to do!' The mouse told himself angrily, for the hundredth time. 'To shake myself out of the window, instead of my duster!'

The mouse, with his head wrapped up in an enormous white bandage, was sitting in the rocking chair by the window in his room. He had been ordered there by the giant, for the doctor had told him that the mouse must have a rest every afternoon, until he was better.

But the mouse was rocking himself hard AWAKE, not asleep. He was not the resting kind of mouse at all. And he couldn't stop thinking how terribly silly he had been.

If it had been the giant who had shaken himself out of the window by mistake, it wouldn't have been so bad. The giant would have laughed it off, and not been hurt. The mouse would have scoffed:

"Huh! Just the sort of thing you *would* do! Daft as a brush!"

But it was not the giant who had done it. It was the mouse. Sensible, careful, organised mouse!

"Everyone must think I'm stupid," he said to the giant, as they sat by the fire that evening, drinking their hot chocolate.

"No, no, of course they don't," said the giant, trying to comfort his friend. "They all know it was a mistake."

"A *stupid* mistake!" cried the mouse, making himself feel even worse.

"If you think your friends have nothing better to do than sit around, thinking how silly you've been, you <u>are</u> silly!" said the giant, sternly. "Now, forget about it and drink up your chocolate. It's your bedtime."

"It's terribly early," complained the mouse. "But I will go up. I feel quite worn out."

"You look it," said the giant.

"Thank you very much," said the mouse, "that makes me feel *much* better!"

"Well, you've been working too hard all day," said the giant, "as usual. And you're not well enough to do it yet. You just won't listen."

"I think I must be getting old, giant," said the mouse, sadly, nibbling a ginger biscuit.

"You're just tired," said the giant. "Now, go to bed. Go on. Off you go."

When the mouse had gone to bed, the giant stayed by the fire for a long time, thinking.

What could he do to make life easier for the mouse?

He had two very good thoughts. First, he must do all the housework and cooking for a while, so that the mouse could relax more. And, second, the mouse must have a day off.

Next day, at breakfast, he talked it over with the mouse.

"As from now, mouse, I think I shall do the cooking and housework. At least until your bandage comes off."

"What, you?" said the mouse. "Good heavens, we'd soon be in a mess. You can't cook. And you're awful at making your bed. You just throw all the covers over, and hope for the best."

"Mouse, it's no use grimble-grumbling at me. You can make your own bed, since you're so fussy about having the sheets all smooth and tucked in tight – I can't reach your rooms, anyway, but THAT'S ALL. And we can live on baked beans, carrots, bread, cheese, apples and milk for a while. It won't hurt us."

The mouse opened his mouth to argue, or be rude, or something, but the giant wouldn't let him speak.

"That's not all," the giant said. "Tomorrow, you're going to spend the day with your Aunt Alice in the village. I'll carry you over in my pocket, and you can have a nicc peaceful time out in the garden with her."

"Aunt Alice! I haven't seen her for ages."

"Exactly," said the giant. "It's time you paid her a visit. She must be wondering what's happened to you."

"That's quite true," agreed the mouse, giving the giant a small smile. "She'll be worried … and it *would* be nice to have the day off."

"Then that's settled," said the giant. And he went out of the kitchen before the mouse could change his mind.

Next day, after he had taken the mouse over to his Aunt Alice's, he came home in one stride, and stood in front of their house.

Where should he start?

He couldn't get into the mouse's rooms. They were much too small. He tidied up his own room, making the bed, sweeping the floor and washing it, putting his clothes away, dusting the shelves, and polishing the table and chair. Then he cleaned the kitchen. He washed up the dishes, swept and washed the floor, opened a can of beans for lunch, and put them ready in the pan. He made a fire, washed the hearth, and looked to see if any shopping had to be done. He stepped across to the village for ten pounds of carrots, and a sack of apples.

By the time he had scrubbed out his own bathroom, cleaned and polished the sitting room and done just a little washing, it was lunchtime.

And the giant was exhausted!

How on earth, he asked himself, does that little mouse do all this, every day of his life? It's a lot for me, but for him – even with the new scooter he whizzes round the house on, it's just too much work. Much, much too much.

The giant allowed himself an hour off. He went down to the field to count buttercups.

But after counting to twenty-three, he dropped off to sleep.

When he woke up, he made himself a nice cup of tea, and sat in the garden. And he did some more thinking.

Something had to be done to make the mouse's life less busy – not just for now, but for always. Nothing came to the giant for a long time. Then suddenly he stood up and shouted: "I've got it!"

The chimney pot jumped off the roof, so great was the noise of the giant's shouting. But the giant, as usual, just put it back in its place, and said, "there, there, poor old chimney", and went on thinking out his plan.

By the time the mouse got home – he had wanted to walk back by himself – the plan was complete.

 "Did you enjoy your day?" the giant asked, over more baked beans at teatime.

"Oh, it was lovely!" said the mouse, looking very bright and cheerful. We had a long chat about things, and a delicious lunch, and then Uncle Cyril took us for a drive."

"I'm so glad, Mousey-mouse," said the giant.

"Yes, and they said they wished I could go with them to the seaside next week. They're spending two weeks at Goldensands. They go every year. Wouldn't that have been nice? But I said I couldn't possibly leave you."

Delighted, the giant listened. He *wanted* the mouse to go away on a holiday. For at least a week. That was part of his plan. Now he didn't even have to ask the mouse if he wanted to go.

"Of course, you can leave me. What is more, you *must!*" said the giant. I mean – I'll be all right."

"Are you sure?" The mouse began to get excited.

"Quite sure," said the giant. "So long as it's not more than two weeks," he added cleverly. After all, he didn't want the mouse to think he wouldn't be missed.

"Won't you be lonely?" asked the mouse.

"Oh, I'll get Uncle Seamus to come over and keep me company," said the giant.

"Oh dear, that awful old wizard!"

"Uncle Seamus is great fun," protested the giant.

"He's bound to do something strange if he comes," said the mouse, doubtfully.

The giant grinned. For that was exactly what he wanted his Uncle Seamus to do. Something very strange indeed …

Chapter 9

FRIENDS AND NEIGHBOURS

Getting the mouse away on holiday was not quite as easy as the giant had thought. The mouse wanted to go – very much indeed. He was very fond of his Aunt Alice and Uncle Cyril. And he was quite sure the mouse would have a splendid time at Goldensands with them.

But there seemed to be so many things to do before he left. First, there were the notes to be written. One for the butcher, one for the baker, one for the farmer – all telling them to leave a very little less meat, bread and milk, until the mouse got back. One for the White mice, telling them not to come and play Snap on Thursday afternoons, for two weeks …

The mouse sat at the kitchen table, with writing paper and envelopes all round him, and it took a whole day to get all the notes off his chest. Then little Terry mouse had to be found to take the notes round to everyone.

The second day was spent packing. The mouse liked to wear the right thing at the right time so, just to be sure, he packed almost all his clothes. He had to wash, iron and air all his shirts first – even those that looked perfectly clean to the giant. And he had to press his blue blazer, and his spotted scarf.

At last, he brought down his big cabin trunk into the garden. He was smartly dressed in a yellow silk shirt, and blue and white spotted jeans. With his sunglasses on, he looked just ready for a holiday.

The giant put the mouse in one pocket, and the cabin trunk in the other, and in one stride they reached Aunt Alice's.'

"Goodbye, giant. Don't forget to –" but the mouse had gone, so the giant never knew what he 'mustn't forget to –'!

He didn't think about it for long, though. He had far more important matters to attend to.

The giant went straight home, and called over Uncle Seamus, who arrived in a puff of violet smoke, and blew himself at the giant to say 'hello'.

"Now, now, Uncle Seamus," coughed the giant, "no silly tricks. I need your help, badly, and it's serious."

The giant explained his plan, and Uncle Seamus nodded, and went straight to work.

Closing his eyes and rubbing his hands together, as if they were cold, Uncle Seamus said, in a high, shrill voice:

"Wind of the whirritty, whirritty woo,
take off this house – and bring back two!
One large, a giant's house,
The other small, right for a mouse."

A sudden gust of whistling wind blew at the house, very hard indeed, and carried it high up, above the woods, into the sky, never to be seen again. And the same wind, still whistling, blew down – in place one house – two houses! There was a large house, like a barn, for the giant. And the other was very small: a mouse cottage.

"Well done, Uncle Seamus!" cried the giant. "Would you like some tea?"

"No no, Aunt Felicity is expecting me home for tea." And with that, Uncle Seamus changed himself quickly into a red feather, which sailed off in the wind.

The giant looked happily at the two houses.

The giant's house was built of yellow brick, with a red-tiled roof and a stone chimney (a chimney that didn't look as though it would jump off as much as the other had done, when the giant shouted!) The mouse's cottage was the same, with a little blue stone chimney sitting on top. It was very pretty indeed.

Now the mouse would not get so tired any more. He could just clean his own house, which had no upstairs windows for him to fall out of, either... The giant would clean his own place, once a month (or whenever he felt like it!). The mouse could still cook for them both, because he liked doing that, in the giant's bed-sitting room, whenever he liked.

It was perfect. The giant was very pleased. Would the mouse be? How could he *not* be?

The giant's next job was to make the two houses ready to live in. He called over the mouse's friends and neighbours and relations, and some of his own.

They set up two camps, on either side of the houses, so that they could work for a week from dawn to nightfall, without having to go home each day.

The giant had never seen so much happening all at once. The mice rushed in and out, first painting the house, then fitting in carpets and furniture, then putting up the curtains with matching covers and cushions. They brought in boxes of new cups, saucers and plates, knives, forks and spoons, tablecloths, napkins and towels. They hung several suitable mousey pictures on the walls.

The giant's Aunt Grace did the same sort of thing with *his* house, helped by quiet Aunt Maud and her three children. The giant and Uncle Seamus just sat at the far end of the garden, watching all the comings and goings, and feeling pleased with themselves.

At night, the mice all got together in the garden. They had supper on the lawn, then sang songs and danced in the moonlight. At midnight, they all went to sleep in their tiny mouse tents and caravans.

The giants made more noise on the other side of the two houses. They were of course much bigger, and spoke much more loudly than the mice. But they all had a very good time, working hard and well by day, and enjoying themselves at night.

At last, all was finished. The mice and giants went home, leaving the giant alone. He unrolled the magic carpet and told it to go very slowly to the mountains, as he had done once before. Just as before, in two minutes he was coming down on the seafront at Goldensands. (The carpet, you'll remember, usually did something quite different from what it was ordered to do.)

The giant told Uncle Cyril and Aunt Alice that he wanted to take the mouse with him on his own, because there was a very special surprise waiting. They quite understood.

"Surprise?" said the mouse, who was looking very brown and bright-eyed after his holiday. "What can it be?"

"Aha, wait and see!" said the giant, with an even bigger smile.

For once, the magic carpet did exactly what the giant risked asking. He took the giant and the mouse straight home. But as they stepped off the carpet, the mouse said:

"That silly carpet! Up to its tricks again! Tell it to take us home, if you dare."

We *are* home!" said the giant, with an even bigger smile.

"No, how can it be? There are two houses here. One big…one – small. Giant, what have you done?"

The mouse walked slowly through the garden until he stood in front of the giant's redbrick house. A little notice, nailed on the front door, read *Giant's Rest*. Then the mouse walked across to the little house. Another, much smaller notice on its front door said *Mouse Cottage*.

The mouse couldn't believe his eyes.

"Go inside and look round your house," begged the giant. "See if you like it, Mousey-mouse."

Turning a golden key in his front door, the mouse went in. His little kitchen was white with red-and-white-checked curtain and tablecloth, and a red-tiled floor. The oak dresser was full of gleaming white cups, saucers and plates, and the stove was hung about with glittering copper pans.

His bathroom was blue, with white tile-fishes stuck all over the walls, and white tiles on the floor, too.

And his bedroom? The mouse gasped with pleasure at what he saw.

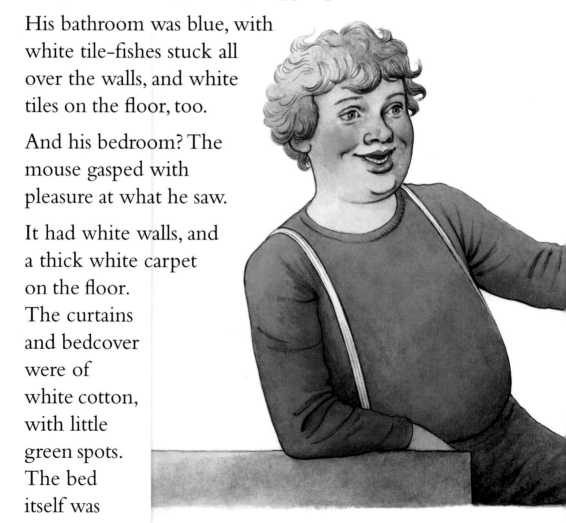

It had white walls, and a thick white carpet on the floor. The curtains and bedcover were of white cotton, with little green spots. The bed itself was made of pinewood; so were the chairs and table, and the dressing table. And, sitting in the window was a new rocking chair, painted white, with a green-spotted white cushion on it.

"My house is – beautiful," murmured the mouse, looking amazed and delighted, as he came out again. "But do we need two houses, giant?"

"Yes," said the giant, "we do. We each need our own place. But we want to be near each other, because we have liked living together. You must only clean *your* house. You can cook for us, if you like, in my house. And you can sit by my fire whenever you want. And – you will never have to do all that work again."

"So now," said the mouse, "we're not just friends."

"No, now we're friends and neighbours," said the giant. "And we're going to live that way, happily ever after."

"Happily ever after?" said the mouse, trying to sound awkward. "Huh, I bet I find something to grumble at!"

And I bet he did, don't you?

THE END